D0571846

Up, Up, Up, Dear Dragon

by Margaret Hillert

Illustrated by David Schimmell

NORWOOD HOUSE PRESS

DEAR CAREGIVER,

The *Beginning-to-Read* series is a carefully written collection of classic readers you may remember from your own childhood. Each book features text comprised of common sight words to provide your child ample practice reading the words that appear most frequently in written text. The many additional details in the pictures enhance the story and offer the opportunity for you to help your child expand oral language and develop comprehension.

Begin by reading the story to your child, followed by letting him or her read familiar words and soon your child will be able to read the story independently. At each step of the way, be sure to praise your reader's efforts to build his or her confidence as an independent reader. Discuss the pictures and encourage your child to make connections between the story and his or her own life. At the end of the story, you will find reading activities and a word list that will help your child practice and strengthen beginning reading skills.

Above all, the most important part of the reading experience is to have fun and enjoy it!

Shannon Cannon,
Literacy Consultant

Norwood House Press • P.O. Box 316598 • Chicago, Illinois 60631
For more information about Norwood House Press please visit our website at
www.norwoodhousepress.com or call 866-565-2900.

LIBRARY OF CONGRESS CATALOGING-IN-PUBLICATION DATA
Hillert, Margaret.
  Up, up, up dear dragon / by Margaret Hillert, illustrated by David Schimmell.
    p. cm. -- (A beginning-to-read book)
  Summary: "A boy and his pet dragon play basketball with friends and learn about good sportsmanship"--Provided by publisher.
  ISBN 978-1-59953-545-6 (library ed. : alk. paper) -- ISBN 978-1-60357-411-2 (ebook)
  [1. Sportsmanship--Fiction. 2. Dragons--Fiction.] I. Schimmell, David, ill. II. Title.
  PZ7.H558Upd 2012
  [E]--dc23
                    2012012629

Manufactured in the United States of America in North Mankato, Minnesota.
                    206N—082012

Father. Father.
Come see this.
See what I can do.

Oh, that looks good.
Do you want to look
for your friends?

6

Oh yes, Father.
I want to look for my
friends so we can play.
Can we?

I know where to go.
There is a good spot
at the school.

7

Here we are.
Here are my friends!
Boys and girls can play this game.

Father, I will go with the red team.
They need me.
Now we will have five to play.

Come on red.
Come on blue.
Let's go.

Go, go, go.
Run, run, run.

Jump up and make it go in.

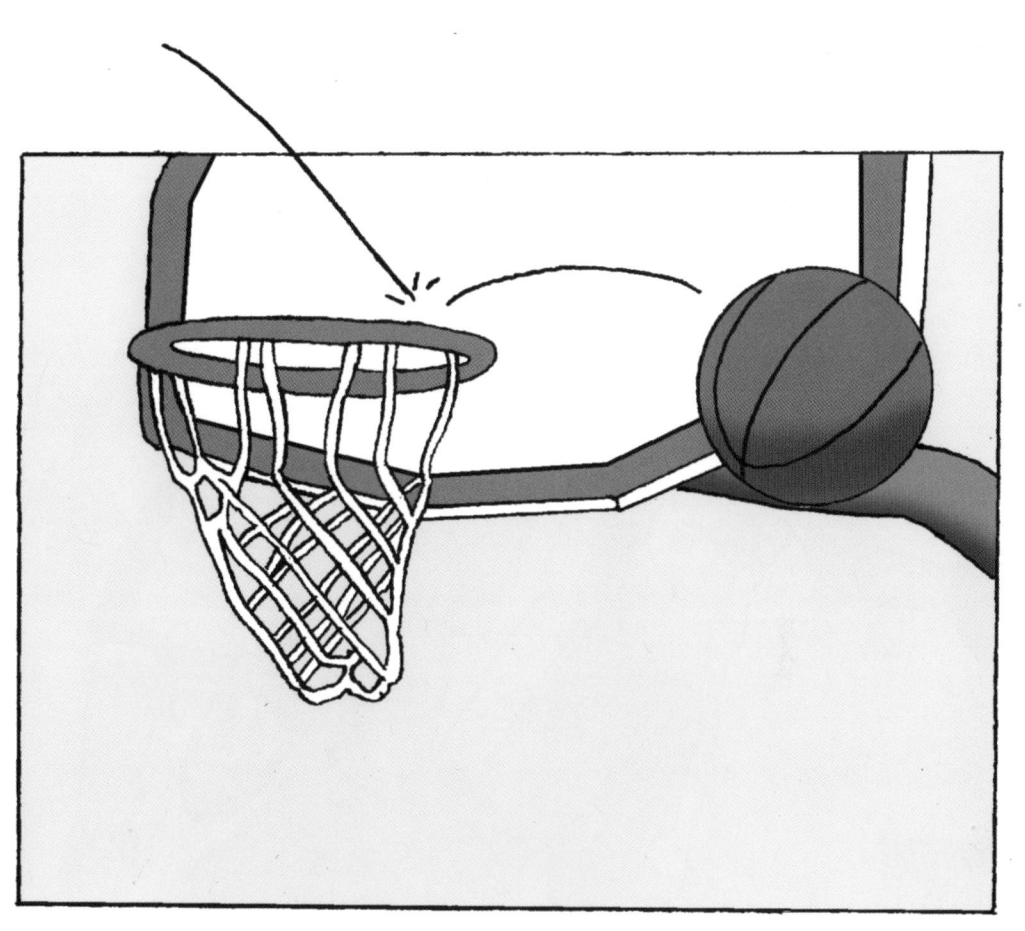

It did not go in.

Now, you go, go, go.
Run, run, run.

Make it go in.
Make it go in.
Up, up, up.

Central

Home of the Dragons

17

That's the way!
That's it.
That's it.

Here we go.
Run, run, run.

Oh h h h h!

20

Get up. Get up.
We have to do this.

Run, run.
Jump, jump, jump!

Oh, good.
You did it.

You are good.
We are good, too.
And we are all good friends.

Now come here.
Look at this.

You will like it.
My Mother makes good cookies.

Dragon you are good, too.
Here you are with me.
And here I am with you.
You are a good friend, Dear Dragon.

The following activities support the findings of the National Reading Panel that determined the most effective components for reading instruction are: Phonemic Awareness, Phonics, Vocabulary, Fluency, and Text Comprehension.

Phonemic Awareness: The /u/ sound

Sound Substitution: Say the words on the left to your child. Ask your child to repeat the word, changing the middle sound to /**u**/:

fin = fun	cap = cup	mad = mud	bat = but
lick = luck	dig = dug	shot = shut	rib = rub
fizz = fuzz	track = truck	bin = bun	rag = rug
snag = snug	lamp = lump	stamp = stump	

Phonics: The letter Uu

1. Demonstrate how to form the letters **U** and **u** for your child.
2. Have your child practice writing **U** and **u** at least three times each.
3. Ask your child to point to the words in the book that have the letter **u** in them.
4. Write down the following words and ask your child to circle the letter **u** in each word:

you	fluff	funny	run	loud	duck
bus	sound	fur	nut	shut	caught
up	such	under	round	plump	pup

Vocabulary: Naming Objects

1. Ask your child to tell you different words he or she thinks of that go with "basketball." Write the words on sticky notes and have the child place them next to any objects he or she has named that are in the story.

2. Ask your child to tell a story using all of the words he or she has come up with that relate to basketball.

Fluency: Shared Reading

1. Reread the story to your child at least two more times while your child tracks the print by tracing a finger under the words as they are read. Ask your child to read the words he or she knows with you.

2. Reread the story taking turns, alternating readers between sentences or pages.

Text Comprehension: Discussion Time

1. Ask your child to retell the sequence of events in the story.

2. To check comprehension, ask your child the following questions:

   - Where do the kids play basketball?
   - What are the two colors of the basketball teams?
   - Who wins the basketball game?
   - What is the final score of the basketball game?
   - What is your favorite game to play? Why is it your favorite?

Up, Up, Up, Dear Dragon uses the 71 words listed below.

This list can be used to practice reading the words that appear in the text. You may wish to write the words on index cards and use them to help your child build automatic word recognition. Regular practice with these words will enhance your child's fluency in reading connected text.

a	father	jump	play	up
all	five			
am	for	know	red	want
and	friend(s)		run	way
are		let's		we
at	game	like	school	what
	get	look(s)	see	where
blue	girls		so	will
boys	go	make(s)	spot	with
	good	me		
can		mother	team	yes
come	have	my	that	you
cookies	here		that's	your
		need	the	
dear	I	not	there	
did	in	now	they	
do	is		this	
dragon	it	oh	to	
		on	too